THE RIG RAN ON

ISBN-13: 978-1-932168-47-1
ISBN-10: 1-932168-47-8
Copyright ©2005 Veritas Press

Veritas Press, Lancaster, Pennsylvania
800-922-5082
www.VeritasPress.com

Second edition

THE RIG RAN ON

STORY BY JOANNA VEITH AND EMILY FISCHER

ILLUSTRATIONS BY JUDITH A. HUNT

The sun was up.
Ed and Gus got up from bed
and ran to Ma and Pa.
They were at the rig.

Pa set a pot, pan and
mop in the rig.
Ma set a rug and a
gun in the rig.

Ed and Gus
fed the dog,
and Pa fit the
bit on the nag.

They were all set to go.

With a pit-pat, pit-pat,
the rig ran on and on
as the red sun set.

When Ma and Pa
and Ed and Gus
got up from bed,
the sun was dim.

Ed and Gus
fed the dog,
and Pa fit the bit
on the nag.

But they were
not all set to go.
The rig was
in the mud!

Pa dug in the mud,
but the mud was wet
and did not let go.

The nag got a pat and a tap.
But the mud was wet.

Ma and Pa and Ed and Gus were sad,
but they were not mad.

They all dug in the mud,
the mud let go,
and the rig got up.

Tap-tap. Tap-tap.
The rig ran on.

When the sun was up,
they met a bad man.

The bad man had a gun and
was set to rob the rig!

Pa got his gun.
With a sob, Ma got
Ed and Gus in the rig.

This was bad. But that was not all.
A red man met them.

Was this red man bad?

The red man was mad
at the bad man.

The bad man ran and ran.

And when the bad man ran,
the red man did go.

With a pit-pat, pit-pat
the rig ran on.
Ma was not sad.
God was with them.

God was with them when
the rig was in the mud.

And God was with them
when they met the bad man.

Tap-tap. Tap-tap. The red sun set.
And the rig ran on.